SCIENCE EXPERIMENTS WITH LIGHT & MIRRORS

GW00985740

Kate Woodward

Designed by Radhi Parekh
Illustrated by Simone Abel
Additional designs: Mary Forster
Consultant: John Baker
Cover design by Russell Punter
Cover illustration by Christyan Fox
With thanks to Sarah Cronin

CONTENTS

Light all around

Light is all around you. Try the experiments in this book to find out more about light and the different ways it behaves.

Sunlight

The Sun is a ball of burning hot gases. It gives off a very bright light. This light travels a distance of 150 million km (93.2 million miles) to reach the Earth.

Moving light

You need a torch for some of the experiments. Switch one on in a dark room.

The light travels away from the torch.

See how the torch lights up things on the other side of the room.

Anything that makes light is called a light source. Light travels from its source to light things up far away.

Making light

How many things can you think of that make light? Here are some to start you off.

Light moves away from a light bulb to light up a room.

Car headlights can light up the road for a long way ahead.

Speedy light

Light is the fastest thing in the universe. It moves at 300,000 km (186,451 miles) a second. It takes only eight and a half minutes to reach Earth from the Sun.

Pictures with the symbol ⌂ can be downloaded from www.usborne-quicklinks.com

Passing through

Collect some things to test whether light can travel through them or not. Here are some you can try.

Foil

Water in glass jug

Velvet

Net curtain

Book

Point a torch at some paper. Hold each thing in front of the torch. Try to guess if it will let light through on to the paper.

Switch on the torch to see if you are right. Make a chart to show what happens with the different things.

You could make your chart like this.

	Light goes through	No light goes through
Foil		
Tissue paper		

Which comes first?

Thunderclouds make lightning and a rumble of thunder at the same time.

You see lightning before you hear thunder because light travels faster than sound.

Different names

Clear things that let light through are called transparent. Things that stop light are called opaque. Some things let light through even though you cannot see through them. These are called translucent.

Glass windows are transparent.

Wooden shutters are opaque.

Most lampshades are translucent.

Internet link Go to *www.usborne-quicklinks.com* for a link to a website where you can do a light and shadows experiment in an online lab.

Travelling light

Although you cannot see it, light is always moving. Here you can find out more about how it travels.

Aiming light

Cover the end of a torch with foil. Make a hole with a pencil so a thin beam of light can shine through.

Push the pencil through the middle of the foil.

Move the torch around. Can you make the beam hit anything you want?

It is easy to aim the beam because the light goes in a straight line.

In the spotlight

Because light travels in straight lines, strong light from theatre spotlights can be aimed at the actors on a stage.

Rays

Each tiny part of light goes along a straight line. These lines are called rays.

This picture shows how rays travel away from a light source.

Bouncing light

Put the foil-covered torch on a table in a dark room. Hold a mirror in front of it. What happens to the beam of light?

Look out for the light spot at the end of the beam. Is it where you expected?

When light hits things, it can bounce off them and travel in a different direction.

You could try using foil or a shiny tin lid instead of a mirror.

Light spot

Try moving the mirror. Can you make the light spot hit different things in the room?

Why is night dark?

The Earth is like a huge ball. It spins around once every 24 hours. For some of the time your part of the Earth faces the Sun and so it is light.

Here it is daytime.

Here it is night.

The sunlight cannot bend around the Earth, so the other side is dark.

How you see

Some light bounces off all the things you see. The light carries a picture of each thing to your eyes.

Light goes to this toy car.

Light rays carry a picture of the car to your eyes.

Looking in mirrors

When you look in a mirror you see your own face. The picture in the mirror is called a reflection.

Finding reflections

Look for different things that you can see your face in. What do you notice about them?

Saucepan

Spoon

Aluminium foil

Glass

Feel each one to find out if it is rough or smooth. Do all the things look shiny?

See if your reflection looks the same in all of them. Is it always the same shape?

New balloon

Seeing a reflection

You see a reflection when light rays bounce off something and on to a mirror.

Light rays

The light rays bounce off the mirror and into your eyes. This makes you see the reflection.

You see the best reflections in things that are flat, shiny and smooth. These make good mirrors.

 Internet link Go to *www.usborne-quicklinks.com* for a link to a website where you can find out more about how mirrors work and try some mirror experiments.

Reflections in water

Look at a puddle on a calm day. It gives a good reflection.

Drop a small pebble in to make ripples in the water. What happens to the reflection?

The light bounces off the ripples in all directions. This makes the reflection disappear.

Glass mirrors

Many mirrors are made of glass. They have a thin layer of silver or aluminium under the glass.

Lots of light bounces off this shiny layer so the mirror gives off a good reflection.

Make an unbreakable mirror

You can use this unbreakable mirror for many of the experiments in this book.

You need: stiff clear plastic*, aluminium foil, stiff cardboard, scissors, sticky tape

1. Cut out rectangles from the foil, the plastic and the cardboard.

Plastic

Foil

Cardboard

Keep the foil smooth.

Make the rectangles all the same size.

2. Put the foil on the cardboard, shiniest side up. Then, put the plastic on top.

3. Put a thin band of tape around the edges to finish it.

*You could use a clear plastic lid from a food container.

Reflections

You do not always see what you expect to see when you look in a mirror. Reflections often look different from real things.

You and your reflection

Look at your reflection in a large mirror. Hold up your left hand.

Watch what happens in the mirror. It's easier if you stand slightly sideways.

Your reflection holds up its right hand. Reflections are always the wrong way around like this. Try other movements to see what happens in the mirror.

Mirror magic

Draw half a circle. Put a mirror along the straight edge.

The mirror shows the half circle back-to-front so it looks like the other half of the circle.

Place your mirror on the dotted lines to complete these three pictures.

Can you draw halves of other things that you can complete with a mirror?

This only works with things that split into two halves exactly the same. Things like this are called symmetrical.

A butterfly is symmetrical.

Internet link Go to www.usborne-quicklinks.com for a link to a website where you can find out why curved funfair mirrors make you look a funny shape.

Funny reflections

Find a large, shiny spoon that can act like a mirror. Look at your face in the back of it.

Mirrors that curve outwards like this are called convex.

Mirrors that curve inwards like this are called concave.

Trick mirrors

Funfairs often use curved mirrors to make people look a funny shape.

Is the reflection the same shape as in a flat mirror?

Now turn the spoon over. What happens to your reflection? Does it change if you bring the spoon closer to your face?

Is the reflection always the same way up?

Curved mirrors even change a reflection's shape. Some can even turn a reflection upside-down.

Secret code writing

This secret code can only be read in a mirror.

You need:
a mirror,
carbon
paper, paper,
a knitting
needle

Plain paper

Carbon paper

1. Lay the carbon paper inky side up. Put plain paper over it. 'Write' on top with the knitting needle.

2. The message appears back-to-front on the other side of the plain paper.

3. Use a mirror to turn the message around so anyone can read it.

meet me at midni

ɘm Ɉɘɘm
Ɉɒ
!Ɉʜǫinbim

Changing reflections

See what happens to the reflections
if you use more than one mirror.

Endless reflections

1. Put two mirrors
face to face and
tape them together.

Put tape down
one edge only.

2. Stand the
mirrors up and put
something small
in between. How
many reflections
can you see?

3. Now move the
mirrors closer
together. Watch
the reflections.

Count the
reflections
now.

As the mirrors
get closer
together, the light bounces from
one to the other and back again.
You see reflections of reflections.

You see most reflections if
you untape the mirrors and
hold them face to face
either side of the object.

Can you count all the
reflections you see?

Making shapes

Tape the mirrors
together again. Put
a pencil in front of
them. Can you make
its reflection form
different shapes?

Open or close the mirrors
to make these shapes.

Triangle	Pentagon	Hexagon
(3 sides)	(5 sides)	(6 sides)

Make a kaleidoscope

Kaleidoscopes use reflections to make colourful patterns.

You will need:
3 rectangular mirrors the same size,
coloured paper cut into tiny shapes,
clear plastic, cardboard,
tracing paper, scissors,
sticky tape, a coloured pencil

1. Tape the long sides of the mirrors together.

The mirrors face each other.

2. Stand the mirrors up on some cardboard. Draw around them and cut out the shape.

3. Tape the cardboard to the mirrors. Push a pencil in the middle to make a hole.

Peephole

Plastic

Tracing paper

4. Draw around the mirrors on the plastic and tracing paper. Cut out the shapes.

You only need a few pieces.

5. Tape two sides of these together to make an envelope. Put the coloured paper inside.

6. Tape up the third side and stick the envelope to the open end of the mirrors.

The tracing paper goes on the outside.

7. Point this end to the light and look through the peephole.

The mirrors reflect the shapes in a pattern. It changes when you shake the kaleidoscope.

Looking around

Mirrors can help you see around corners and in awkward places. Here you can find out how.

Looking behind

Hold a mirror in front of you. Can you see anything else besides your reflection?

Try moving the mirror slightly to one side.

You can see things behind you because light bounces off them and on to the mirror.

Ask a friend to move around behind you. Can you always see her reflection in the mirror?

You have to tilt the mirror to see your friend in different places.

Make a periscope

This shows you how to use mirrors to make a periscope.

You will need:
a long, thin cardboard box,
2 small mirrors the same size,
scissors,
sticky tape

1. Ask an adult to cut matching slits in two opposite sides of the box, as shown. Do this near the top and the bottom.

The slits must slant like this.

Useful mirrors

Drivers use mirrors to help them see other traffic on the road behind them.

Internet link Go to **www.usborne-quicklinks.com** for a link to a website where you can find more fun activities with light and reflections.

Cut the window in the side nearest the top of the slits.

2. Cut a window level with the top slits. Slide a mirror though the slits so the shiny side faces the window. Tape it in place.

3. Cut another window, this time level with the bottom slits on the opposite side of the box. Slide a second mirror through the slits and fasten it with tape.

The shiny side of the mirror faces the window.

4. Point the periscope over a wall. Look through the bottom window. What can you see?

How it works

You can see things over the wall because light from them travels to the top mirror.

Light bounces from one mirror to another inside the box.

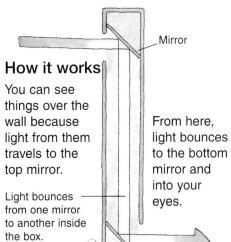

Mirror

From here, light bounces to the bottom mirror and into your eyes.

Up periscope

The crew of a submarine can see what is happening above the surface by raising a periscope out of the water.

The light carries pictures down to the crew.

Tricks of light

Light can play some surprising tricks on your eyes. You cannot always believe what you see.

Straight or bent?

Put a straw in a glass of water. Look down on it from above. What happens to the straw?

The straw looks bent at the surface of the water.

Try other straight things to see if they look bent too.

Light travels more slowly through water than through air. As it slows down, it changes direction. This can make things in water look bent when they are really straight.

Appearing coin

Stick a coin to the bottom of a bowl with tape. Look over the edge of the bowl, then move back until you just cannot see the coin anymore.

Keep still and ask a friend to pour water into the bowl. What happens?

When the bowl is empty, the edge of the bowl stops you seeing the coin.

When the bowl is full, the light bends over the edge, so you can see the coin.

Internet links Go to **www.usborne-quicklinks.com** for links to websites where you can try more light tricks and find out why magnifying glasses make things look bigger.

Changing shape

Collect some things that you can see through. Hold them in front of a book. What happens to the words?

Try some of these things.

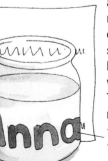

The words look a different shape because light bends when it passes through any clear object.

Ruler
Ice
Marble
Pair of glasses

The amount it bends depends on the shape of the object.

Fill a clean glass jar with water and stand it in front of the page. The jar and the water make a solid curved shape. This shape bends the light to make the words look bigger. This is called magnification.

The words look bigger through the jar.

In the swim

A swimming pool looks shallower than it really is because of the way light is bent through water. This also makes your legs look short and fat.

Magnifying glass

A magnifier is made of a piece of solid curved glass called a lens. The lens makes light bend just as a jar of water does.

This lens has been cut in half so you can see how it is curved.

Microscope

Lenses are used in microscopes to make tiny things look many times bigger.

Making pictures

Photographs are pictures made by light rays. Here you can find out how light can make pictures and how light helps you to see pictures too.

Make a pinhole camera

Light can make pictures appear for a moment inside this camera.

1. Cut out the top of the box, then paint the inside black. Let the paint dry. Tape tracing paper over the opening.

You need:
a cardboard box, black paint and paintbrush, tracing paper, sticky tape, scissors, a pin, a dark cloth

The pictures will appear on this tracing paper screen.

2. Use a pin to push a tiny hole in the box, opposite the tracing paper screen.

3. Go outside. Hold the screen up to your eyes. Ask a friend to put a cloth over your head and around the sides of the box.

Point the hole at different things to get a picture on the screen. Do you see anything surprising?

Hole

How the pictures appear

Light rays bounce off things and carry a picture through the pinhole on to the screen.

Light rays

Pinhole

Screen

The rays cross over as they pass through the pinhole, so the pictures appear upside-down.

Internet link Go to *www.usborne-quicklinks.com* for a link to a website where you can watch an animated explanation of how eyes work.

Taking photographs

Real cameras have film at the back instead of a screen.

When you press a button, a shutter lets light in. The light marks a picture on the film. This can be printed on to paper to make a photograph.

Film

Shutter

Light goes in here

The shutter can open and close.

How your eyes see pictures

Your eye works a little like a pinhole camera. A hole at the front, called the pupil, lets light in.

The light carries a picture to the back of the eye. This part is called the retina.

This shows the inside of the eye.

Retina

Pupil

This picture is upside-down. Your brain turns it around so that you see things the right way up.

Looking at eyes

Stand in a dim room for a few minutes and look at your eyes in a mirror. Look closely at your pupils. Then put the light on. See how your pupils change size.

In dim light pupils open up to let more light in so you can see more.

In bright light pupils close up to stop too much light damaging your eyes.

17

The colour of light

Most light looks clear or white, but it is really a mixture of different colours.

Make your own rainbow

You can make the different colours appear like this.

Stand with your back to the Sun and spray water from a hose. What colours can you see in the spray?

Look into the spray against a dark wall or hedge.

Colour wheel

You can make colours change with this spinning colour wheel.

You need:
cardboard, a jar,
coloured crayons,
scissors, a pencil,
ruler

1. Draw around the bottom of a jar to make a circle. Cut the circle out.

Light bends as it goes through the water. Each colour of light bends by a different amount so you see each one separately. The bands of coloured light make a rainbow.

Rainbow colours

A rainbow appears in the sky when the Sun shines through rain. The same colours always appear in the same order.

Violet
Indigo
Blue
Green
Yellow
Orange
Red

Follow this as a colour guide.

2. Divide the circle into seven roughly equal parts. Colour each part a different rainbow colour.

3. Push a sharp pencil through the middle of the circle. Spin it quickly on a table. Watch what happens to the colours on the card.

Different colours of light bounce off each part of the wheel. As the wheel spins, these merge to make one very pale colour.

Coloured things

Most things only let some colours of light bounce off them. You can see the colours as they bounce off.

This red pepper looks red because only red light bounces off it.

If all the colours bounce off something, you see them mixed together. This mixture looks white.

This hanky looks white because all the colours bounce off it.

Changing colour

Collect some see-through sweet wrappers in different colours. Look at some white paper through each one. Does the paper always look white?

All the colours of light bounce off the paper, but each wrapper only lets its own colour through. This makes the paper look the same colour as the wrapper.

Light and shadow

Whenever there is light, things
have shadows. Here you can
find out how shadows happen.

This
works
best in
a dark
room.

Is the shadow always
the same shape and
size as your hand?

Making shadows

Put a torch on a
chair and shine it
at a wall. Put your
hand in front.
What do you see
on the wall?

A shadow shows where
your hand blocks the light
and stops it reaching the wall.

Make different shapes with your hand.
See what happens to the shadow.

Sun shadows

Things outside have
shadows because they
keep sunlight from
reaching the ground.

Go outside with a
friend on a sunny
day. Measure each
other's shadows at
different times. Does
your shadow stay
the same length?

When the Sun
is high you only
block out a few
rays of light so
your shadow
is short.

All shadows are short
at midday, when the
Sun is high in the sky.

When the Sun is low
you block out more
rays of light and so
your shadow is long.

Shadows are longer in
the morning and evening,
when the Sun is low.

Internet link Go to www.usborne-quicklinks.com *for a link to a website where you can
find out how to use shadows for measuring - and measure a dinosaur!*

Make a shadow theatre

1. Cut the top and bottom out of a cardboard box. Cut a slot in each side, as shown.

Slots

Give your shadow show in a dark room.

2. Cut out cardboard shapes for puppets. Tape each one to a ruler.

Move the puppets to make the shadows act out a story.

3. Tape tracing paper over one end of the box. Push the puppets through the slots. Shine a light behind the puppets to make their shadows appear.

Shadow clock

Early on a sunny morning, push a stick firmly into the ground. Put a stone at the end of the stick's shadow.

Write the time on the stone with chalk.

See where the shadow is after an hour. Mark the shadow again with another stone. Do this every hour until late afternoon.

The shadow moves because the Sun moves across the sky. The shadow always falls on the side of the stick which is away from the Sun.

The next day you can tell the time by seeing which stone the shadow is on.

The stones show how the shadow moves.

21

How the experiments work

These pages give more detailed explanations of how some of the experiments in the book work. To find out even more about the experiments, visit the websites recommended. For links to all these websites, go to **www.usborne-quicklinks.com**

Travelling light (pages 4-5)

Light rays are given off from all light sources. They spread out as they go. Objects further away from a source are less brightly lit than those close to it because fewer rays hit the same surface area.

Light source

Light rays

*Internet link Go to **www.usborne-quicklinks.com** for a link to a website where you can find out more about how light travels.*

Safety with mirrors

It is safer to put tape around the edges and across the back of a glass mirror. This stops pieces of glass from scattering if the mirror breaks.

Reflections (pages 8-9)

The way light rays bounce off a mirror affects the way you see the image, or reflection, in the mirror.

Light rays bouncing off a flat mirror.

When light rays hit a flat mirror head on, they bounce straight back. The image looks the same size as the object.

When light rays hit a concave mirror they bounce inwards so they cross. This makes the image look upside-down, unless you are very close to the mirror.

Light rays bouncing off a concave mirror.

A convex mirror makes light rays bounce outward. This makes the image look smaller than the real object.

Light rays bouncing off a convex mirror.

*Internet link Go to **www.usborne-quicklinks.com** for a link to a website where you can discover how light reflects off smooth and rough surfaces.*

Changing reflections (pages 10-11)

The smaller the angle between two mirrors, the more light can bounce between them. This results in more reflections. In theory, you can see an infinite number of reflections from a point between two parallel mirrors. In real life, this is impossible because you cannot stand between the mirrors without getting in the way of the reflected light.

Tricks of light (pages 14-15)

The way light rays change direction as they travel from one material (such as air or water) to another is known as refraction.

Magnifiers

Real object

Magnifying glass

Eye

Image that you see.

The angle of the rays makes the object look larger than it really is.

Rays of light reflected from an object are bent inward as they go through a magnifying lens. The angle of the rays travelling into your eye causes the image you see to look bigger than the object.

Making pictures (pages 16-17)

The picture inside the pinhole camera may be blurred because the rays from a particular point of an object do not hit the screen at the same place. In modern cameras (and in the human eye) a lens bends so that rays coming from any one point on the object meet to form a clear image.

Lens

Light rays

The colour of light (pages 18-19)

Different colours of light bounce off different parts of the spinner. As it turns, they mix into one colour. This looks near-white, not pure white, because the colours of the crayon on the spinner are not exactly the same as those of light.

Internet link Go to *www.usborne-quicklinks.com* *for a link to a website where you can discover what happens when you mix coloured light.*

Light and shadow (pages 20-21)

The shadow clock only tells the time accurately for a few days. This is because the relative positions of the Earth and the Sun slowly change throughout the year. This gradually changes the place where the shadow falls at a given time.

Index

First published in 2002 by Usborne Publishing Ltd., Usborne House, 83-85 Saffron Hill, London EC1N 8RT, England.
www.usborne.com Copyright © 2002, 1993 Usborne Publishing Ltd. The name Usborne and the device ♀ (☺) are Trade Marks of Usborne Publishing Ltd. All rights reserved. No part of this publication may be reproduced, stored in a retrieval system, or transmitted in any form or by any means, electronic, mechanical, photocopying, recording, or otherwise, without the prior permission of the publisher. Printed in China.